P9-BYK-341

MONSTER NIGHT AT GRANDMA'S HOUSE

Richard Peck

Illustrated by

Don Freeman

Richard Peck

Dial Books for Young Readers  New York

A Note from the Author

Back in the 1970's when I was starting out as a writer for young readers, I did my only story for the very young—my only picture book.

I showed the story, *Monster Night at Grandma's House,* to my Viking Press publisher, George Nicholson. To my surprise, he decided that Viking would take it. Then he said, "If you could have any artist in the world to do the illustrations, who would it be?"

Without hesitation, or much hope, I said, "Don Freeman."

How well I recall that moment when George Nicholson said, "We can ask him."

We did, and Don said he'd like to illustrate my story, but his own books came first in his working schedule. I'd have to wait, and I said I'd wait as long as it took. It took two years.

I was willing to rewrite Toby's story to conform to Don's illustrations, but I don't remember the changing of a word. What I do remember is traveling to Santa Barbara to see the work in progress. Don and his wife, Lydia, lived in a sort of dream of how artists ought to live. Their house, high in the trees, was a series of bungalows, vaguely Asian, arranged along a catwalk: a studio for him, a study for her, a house for entertaining, above the town against a backdrop of blue Pacific.

I'd said I'd wait as long as it took for Don Freeman to illustrate *Monster Night at Grandma's House.* I might have waited forever because Don died soon after, too soon. And so our book was one of his last.

More than a quarter of a century later, Toby's intrepid visit to Grandma's house is still spurring me on. Two books of mine for somewhat older readers, *A Long Way from Chicago* and *A Year Down Yonder,* won the silver and gold John Newbery medals in 1999 and 2001. And what are they about? Two grandkids go off to visit Grandma in her tall and shadowy domain—a big old lady in a big old house full of history and mystery. Now if only Don were here to add the brushwork.

Richard Peck
2003

Grandma's house was perfect during the day. Toby could swoop out on the porch swing, right over the rail and the snowball bushes.

He wasn't scared a bit, no matter how high the swing went or how loud it squawked.

Out behind the garage where Grandma parked her Plymouth Duster there was a fish pond. It was all dried up, and the fish were gone. But Toby would carry buckets of water to fill it. Sometimes he even did a little fishing before the water seeped through the cracks in the bottom. Toby had a lot of good ideas like that.

Last August when Toby visited Grandma's house, there was one row of sweet corn along the fence, as usual. The corn leaves rustled and whispered in the warm wind. He and Grandma had corn on the cob, dripping with butter, just about every night.

But after supper, things at Grandma's house always changed. Bath time wasn't bad. In fact, it was good. But when he had to get out and put on his pajamas, like tonight, Toby knew trouble was just around the corner.

"Come and kiss my wrinkled face before you go to bed," Grandma said.

So Toby did, though her face was hardly wrinkled at all. Just a couple of little places around her eyes behind her glasses. He wanted to crawl up in her lap. She wanted him to. But they both knew he was getting too big for that.

"Bedtime now. Big day tomorrow," Grandma said. She said that every night because all the days at her house were big days. The trouble was, the nights were long. The days were just the right size. The nights weren't.

So, just as he did every August night, Toby climbed the tall stairs, counting the steps. Fourteen to the landing. Turn left. Turn left again. Seven steps more to the upstairs hall. Eight giant steps to the front room where Toby slept.

Everything was wrong with that room. There was only a little light from outside to show Toby the way. It was five giant steps to the creaking board that he hated. Then five more giant steps to the bed. The bed was too high, too wide, too long, and entirely too lonely.

The worst part was . . . Grandma slept downstairs.

Even on a night as hot as this one, Toby pulled up the scrap quilt. Sometimes when he was lucky, he'd fall asleep before he could hear the little click downstairs as Grandma switched off her reading lamp.

But on nights as bad as this one, he heard her lamp click off. Grandma would soon be fast asleep, far away.

Then he heard the night bugs hitting the window screen. The longer he listened, the more those bugs sounded like fingers. Some were little tapping fingers. Some were big poking fingers. And some were scratching fingers that didn't sound a bit like bugs.

On this worst night of all, that floorboard creaked. Toby knew there were no such things as monsters. Besides, he was brave for his age. He wanted to sit right up in bed and say,

"WHO'S THERE AND WHAT DO YOU WANT?"

Instead, he just lay there waiting, the scrap quilt pulled right up to his shut-tight eyes.

Why didn't that floorboard creak again? If it creaked once, why didn't it creak twice? There could only be one reason:

SOMEBODY OR SOME *THING* WAS STANDING ON IT.

It was a tough situation. All at once Toby found it hard to breathe. With his eyes shut tight, it was darker than night.

And someone or some *thing* was standing only five giant steps from his bed, on that board.

Toby didn't mean to, but he fell asleep after Creak Number One. But that was a dangerous thing to do—this falling asleep with maybe a Monster practically at his toes. So he woke up again right away. It was hard to sleep with the scrap quilt over his nose. He tried to take short quick breaths so that the quilt wouldn't move and give him away.

If the Monster didn't see anything stirring, it might think Toby was only a pillow.

He started listening again for the telltale second creak—Creak Number Two. He waited a long time. It felt like a couple or three hours. The longer he waited, the harder it was to breathe. So he held his breath.

But he was still almost positive he could hear breathing. Not *his* breathing. Different breathing. It was definitely not far off, and it was of two kinds. Breathing in and breathing out. Monster breathing.

If he could only see a little light, it would mean the Monster was the fire-breathing kind. Maybe the flames were shooting right over his bed. He squeezed up his eyes hard to see through the shut-tight lids.

He began to see lights. Little green stars at first. Then pale orange lightning. Then little squares of all colors, like Grandma's scrap quilt, but brighter.

Only a Monster could breathe out all those fire colors. Suddenly Toby felt hot. No wonder, since the Monster was heating up the room with long flame breaths.

Toby was beginning to enjoy looking at the colors seeping through his eyelids. But that floorboard creaked again. Loud. It echoed, scaring all the finger-bugs off the window screen.

Toby didn't like to open his eyes in bed, but he had to know what was going on. It was dark out there in the room. The fire-breathing Monster was gone, and it had taken its fire with it. The room was still hot, though. A few of the finger-bugs came back to bang against the screen.

The Monster couldn't be far off. It was probably just outside the door. Toby could almost hear it breathing—snorting, in fact. He pushed the scrap quilt down a little. He took a few deep swallows of night air. The room seemed to be cooling off. He looked around the empty room.

Why did it leave? Toby thought for a while.

Maybe the Monster is scared of ME! This was a new idea for Toby. *Maybe now I've got him on the run!*

Suddenly, Toby saw two strange lumpish shapes halfway down his bed. They worried him until he saw they were only his two feet. He wiggled his toes just to check this out, and grinned in the dark.

Then he saw the doorway into the hall. Had he left that door open or closed? It was open now. Maybe some *thing* was just about to crawl back into the room.

Everything went quiet. Bugs. Floorboards. The whole world listened while Toby stared at the black shape of the doorway.

He noticed something out on the hall floor. A gray shape against the blackness. Could it be one of Grandma's rag-rugs? No, it was the wrong shape. Tiny at one end and wider at the other. Toby fastened his eyes on it. Maybe it moved a little. Maybe it didn't. Yes, it did! No. He couldn't be sure.

Toby slid cautiously over to the edge of the bed. He kept a close watch on that gray shape on the hall floor. When he moved, it moved. When he stopped, it stopped.

His feet were hanging over the side when he knew what that shape was:

IT WAS THE MONSTER'S TAIL.

The Monster was probably all humped over just around the corner of the door . . . waiting. Or if it was the type with an extra-long tail, it might be all the way over to the stairs.

Toby took a giant step and stopped. The Monster's tail moved an inch. Toby took another giant step.

The tail moved two inches. Toby landed right on the creaking floorboard. When it creaked, the Monster's tail twitched once and was gone.

Toby stood right on the footprints of the Monster. The floorboard was still warm from Monster paws. Toby stepped onto a cooler floorboard, heading toward the black doorway.

The only thing he could hear was the rest of the night world listening. And maybe just the sly sound of the Monster creeping downstairs. He listened with all his might.

There was only a velvety sound as the Monster's claws scratched down the steps. There was a quieter sound than this as the Monster's tail thumped down behind it. Toby moved toward the doorway. The velvety scratch-and-thump was fading fast. Toby was almost afraid he'd miss some *thing*. So he stretched his head around the door and scanned the hall with one eye.

He saw a spot, bright as a star. It was an eye. AN EYE. Toby looked at the eye with his eye. They stared, eye-to-eye.

The eye was Monster-big, and it glittered like glass. In fact, it *was* glass. Toby was pleased with himself because he knew right off this was only the moose head's eye. That old moth-eaten moose head was always there, and never moved.

Toby didn't like being looked at by a moose head. Still, it was better than being breathed on by a night-crawling, flame-throwing, tail-thumping sneak of a Monster. Anything's better than that.

Toby was as silent as the moose head. He heard no more scratching and thumping from the stairs. The Monster was already down below. But where, for Pete's sake? He stared and stared down into the shadows. There it was, practically as plain as day. The tail was sliming its wicked way along the downstairs hall floor. It moved only when Toby moved, which was clever. But Toby saw through this trick.

But maybe the Monster didn't even know it was being followed. Or maybe it didn't know how brave Toby was. Monsters don't know everything.

It had crept into the parlor. Maybe it was leaving the house. Maybe it had some more stops to make that night. Maybe Toby might as well go back to bed. He needed the rest.

But he also needed to know where that Monster was going. So he crept on down to the front hall. The parlor was quiet. But there were rugs in there, a lot of them. Needle-sharp Monster claws could sink into them without a sound. Forked and scaly tails of any length could whip quietly across those rugs with no more than a husky whisper.

The parlor could be full of Monsters with whispering tails, dripping fangs, rolling red eyes, fiery nostrils—you name it—and still be as silent as a snowfall.

Toby marched through the double doors anyway, his heart pounding, but brave. He told his feet to steal without stumbling over the deep rug, toward the long window.

There was a squeaking sound out on the porch. Like a family of mice scooped up suddenly in a Monster mouth. Either that or the Monster was hoisting its awful, oozy, shapeless great hulking body up over the porch rail and down under the big flowers of the snowball bushes.

What big waddling, wall-eyed, tongue-lolling Monster would just stroll off down the front walk like everyday people?

Were the snowball bushes nodding in the night breeze? Or were they nodding because the Monster was slithering down among their roots?

To keep an eye on the action, Toby eased up into the porch swing. He sat there as still as a pillow to keep the swing from squawking. He let out a big sigh. Maybe it had taken half the night, but he'd chased that THING off the place. Toby felt as brave as an astronaut. Possibly braver.

If he stayed very quiet, maybe he could see the Monster lumbering and lurching and snorting down the street. There'd be no more trouble at Grandma's house that night. Maybe never again. He closed his eyes to give them a rest so they could keep watch later.

But before he could get his eyes open, he heard the terrifying swish of a mean, scaly tail. That blasted Monster hadn't learned its lesson after all. It was on the way back. The crunchy brushing sound was far off at first. But it got louder.

Toby jerked to attention, making the swing chains rattle. The light needling his eyes was blinding bright. Brilliant rays of yellow and white, like Monster-breath fire. The snowball flowers glowed. It was daytime. The dark shapes and slipping shadows were gone.

But the terrible scaly swishing wasn't. It came nearer, along the side of the house and up the steps and right onto the porch.

But the swishing was only Grandma's big broom. She was stepping along behind it, making the leaves and ragweed pollen fly. Toby slumped back and let out a big whistle of relief.

"My stars!" Grandma said. "What in the world?"

"Everything's okay, Grandma," Toby told her. "It was here, but now it's gone. I took care of it. There's not a thing in the world to worry about. Not around here anyway."

"Well, I'm certainly glad to hear it," Grandma said. "Now, hot cereal for you, and plenty of it. It's going to be a big day!"

Toby slipped out of the swing. He took one last look at the porch rail.

There right on the top of it he saw one perfect Monster-paw print. Three terrible toe-prints dotted at the tops with three nasty claw prints. THE MARKS OF THE MONSTER. Clear as day.

"It was a big night too, Grandma!" Toby said. He followed her in to breakfast, braver than ever.

For ROZELLA and HERBERT BOTTRELL
and their grandchildren
ANDREW and JILL BOTTRELL

and this new edition is for SPENCER BYERS

Published by Dial Books for Young Readers 2003
A division of Penguin Putnam Inc.
345 Hudson Street
New York, New York 10014

First published by The Viking Press 1977

Text set in Trump Mediaeval
Manufactured in China on acid-free paper

1 3 5 7 9 10 8 6 4 2

Library of Congress Cataloging-in-Publication Data
Peck, Richard, date.
Monster night at Grandma's house / Richard Peck ; illustrated by Don Freeman.
p. cm.
Summary: Daytime at Grandma's house is fine, but bedtime is terrifying
when a monster seems to be about.
ISBN 0-8037-2904-9
[1. Night—Fiction. 2. Monsters—Fiction. 3. Grandmothers—Fiction.
4. Bedtime—Fiction.]
I. Freeman, Don, 1908–1978, ill. II. Title.
PZ7.P338 Mo 2003 [E]—dc21 2002015606

The drawings were done with India ink
on scratchboard, with a watercolor overlay.